CURSES, CATS & CORPSES

A Charmed Cocktail Cozy

M. L. BONATCH

Cover Art by Spellbinding Designs

Editor: Three Point Author Services

Proofreader: Y.K. Bonatch

CURSES, CATS & CORPSES

A Charmed Cocktail Cozy Mystery

Book 1

ABOUT THIS BOOK

Her magic might not be up to par, but she's no killer. The question is, who is?

Marissa Hale dreams of making her mark as a charmed cocktail mixologist. But her mediocre magic skills have her putting her aspirations on ice and moving in at Gran's retirement community. And just as she's acclimating to the resident nosey witches, she's horrified when a trip to the work freezer offers up a corpsesicle.

Her resentful vampire coworker insists Marissa is a prime suspect since her hair has a new dark shade, implying a recent magical mishap. Admitting she's been secretly practicing her cocktails and a misfire caused the color—and the ability to talk to a cat—would only stir up more trouble.

Will Marissa's best shot at finding the culprit be enough to keep her from getting served a murder charge?

Curses, Cats & Corpses is the bewitching first book in the Charmed Cocktail Cozy mystery series. Raise your glass if you like quirky characters, furry sidekicks, and amateur sleuthing.

"I need to go inside before I melt into this lounge chair." I fanned my face using a magazine with headlines boasting spells for halting aging and potions to extend your familiar's life. Since I was only twenty-eight and had yet to develop a magical connection with a familiar—even though I'd tried exhaustively with my shih tzu—the magazine was more useful as a fan. "Mulder and I aren't used to Florida's heat."

I patted the panting little fur ball who looked up at me with huge, brown eyes. Like me, Mulder was more comfortable in the cool temperatures of Pennsylvania. This trip to Florida had sounded perfect. Pennsylvania was having a winter like they hadn't seen in ages—and I'd lost my job.

"Stay put, Marissa. You'll get used to the heat."

Gran waved me off as she slathered more suntan lotion on her arms while her loose skin tried to evade her efforts.

Maybe I would, but I wasn't sure I'd get used to the current view here at the pool. I'd missed my grandmother since she'd moved into the retirement community, but I hadn't planned on staying with her, or being visually traumatized by half-naked, hairy, geriatric warlocks who seemed intent on making me consider stabbing out my own eyeballs.

"Why do they have to wear those tiny swimsuits? Haven't they ever heard of swim trunks?" I turned to my gran where she sat soaking up the rays of sun like she was immune to skin cancer. Technically, since she was a witch, she was mostly immune, but there was still something to be said about protecting a fair complexion. I tilted my large sunhat to shield my face from the rays and avoid morphing into the color of cotton candy. A raging sunburn would clash with my bright pink hair.

Gran shrugged, took a sip of her tropical drink complete with a tiny umbrella, and adjusted the strap on the teeny, flowered bikini even I'd be uncomfortable wearing in public. "Why not? You should be happy Henry and Fred are wearing anything. They've both been vying for Charlotte's attention. If you stick around for a while, you'll get to experience second

Saturday skinny-dipping." She waggled her penciled-in eyebrows.

I cringed and made a mental note to make myself scarce if I was still around then. I didn't plan to be, but I also hadn't planned to stay this long. Without a job waiting at home, it wasn't like I had any reason to hurry back.

"Relax and live a little." Gran slid down her jeweled cat eye sunglasses to inspect the warlock strutting past, giving us an eyeful of sights I couldn't unsee. "You youngsters spend too much time worrying about what everyone thinks."

"Ava says I should worry more." It was hard to be a good witch and live up to expectations when your fraternal twin sister was perfect. Even though we looked nothing alike, I had a constant reminder of the witch I could be if I followed all the rules of etiquette and started giving a crapola about the opinions of others. Which meant, you know, giving up everything that made me, me.

"Nonsense. I love you and your sister equally, but you remind me of myself at your age." She lifted a hand mirror and began applying dark red lipstick. Once finished, she sat the mirror and lipstick on the small wicker table between us.

I hadn't informed my sister that I'd lost my latest job. Gran was the only one who knew about that. I wasn't up for a lecture from. "So you were unemployed most of that time, too?" I raised a brow.

She ignored my sarcastic response. I'd told those who'd asked that I was between jobs, but this was Gran. I could be honest with her. Despite having a degree in hospitality, the best job I could maintain was a cocktail waitress. Truth be told, I preferred mixing the cocktails rather than just serving them. I was good at it. Well... usually.

I lifted the mirror to scan my hair in case a new dark streak had shown up. These streaks usually indicated that the witch had done a nasty spell. With me, they showed up when I did a spell badly, not when I did a wicked spell. It was pretty unfair that a witch's hair advertised mis-spelling like a scarlet letter of shame if they didn't have the money, or the spell savvy, to keep any embarrassing streaks covered.

I was sure the rest of the supernatural community did more than their share of misdeeds, except it did not force them to advertise it. Instead, they just looked down their judgmental noses at us, or at least at me.

I ran my hand over my locks. "I need a touch up. People will talk if my hair color isn't consistent, or if I get a dark streak. I don't want to embarrass you around your friends." Willow Hill's witch and warlock condominiums were a hot commodity. Gran had waited years for a spot; I didn't want to get her kicked out.

The woman who'd served as my mentor and role model for most of my life reached behind her to unwedge her bikini bottom. "If you're worrying about embarrassing me, you're wasting your time. I'm long past that."

She had a point there.

"Besides, your hair looks fine."

"Easy for you to say." I glanced at Gran's snow white hair. Not a streak to be seen. That's because she was exceptional at spelling and never had to worry about magical mishaps unexpectedly showcased in her stylish locks.

"I worry because I don't have extra cash for a trip to the salon." I'd lost yet another hairdresser. They either couldn't keep up with the frequency of touchups I needed, or they couldn't keep their mouth shut about it. A witch's hair was sacred and the touch up but shut up rule was an unspoken one. At least it was until some of the darn hairdressers' tongues started wagging.

My stylist had covered the streak and then flapped her gums to anyone who'd listened about the particular spell that had brought me in for a visit. Nobody would understand that I'd only wanted to get Tristan to see me, really see me. And he saw me, I suppose, when I'd showed up to our first and only date with a black streak in my hair. Shortly after, he'd learned for himself how I'd received the accessory when an extra eye sprouted from his forehead during dinner.

My humiliation couldn't match Tristen's annoy-ance, which was understandable. Even after I reversed the spell, he never looked at me the same way again. I admit I might've acted harshly by charming my hairdresser's coffee for telling that secret to everyone who'd listen. If only I'd considered that the security cameras could catch me in the act. When questioned, I'd insisted it was only to make her regret her actions and learn to keep her trap shut. The coffee charm may have also come with a side effect of explosive diarrhea. Honestly, that wasn't my intent.

Another bridge burned before I'd left for my trip.

Gran forced me from my musings. "Here's a thought. Why not get a job while you're here? Maybe the club down the street, Night Moves, is hiring. You're a great cocktail waitress and you should be able to make better money here than you do at home." She held up a hand. "Just don't introduce any of your charmed cocktail recipes right away. Those are trouble. I'm not sure their bartender would be receptive. He's kind of odd. Take some time to fit in and let them get to know and love you before offering your specialty drinks."

"Night club? You mean the bar that looks like a rundown hole in the wall?"

Gran shrugged. "You should know better than to judge anything, or anyone, by appearance. The owner keeps the club glamorized to discourage normals from stopping in."

I frowned, wondering if she was referring to more than the club with the whole "don't judge by appearances" speech. I hadn't shared the story about my last hairdresser, but she knew of plenty of other minor magical mishaps I'd inadvertently been responsible for over the years.

"How in the world could a nightclub do well this close to a retirement community?" Paranormals comprised most of the adjoining small town. Though quaint, the area didn't look like a place that would provide much in tips.

"You know that the lifespan of paranormals is much longer than normals. The older we get, the more we want to have fun and enjoy every bit of life left in our years." She winked and inclined her head toward the two warlocks chatting with a few witches. "Look at Henry and Fred. They know they're not dead yet, and I can bet Charlotte is going to make the most of that."

I sighed and put the mirror down. "Fine. I'll put in an application." It was actually a good idea. I wasn't ready to go home yet, but I could only stay with Gran for a limited time. Apparently, there was an age limit, and I didn't meet it for multiple decades.

"Great. But don't worry. I don't mind if you crash here for the summer," she said.

"Who said anything about the summer?" I was thinking of an extra few weeks to delay the inevitable when I would have to tell Ava the truth about my impromptu trip.

"Why not? Where else are you going to get to enjoy all this?" She expanded her arms to encompass the clear blue sky and sweltering sun, then lowered them to remind me that there were six other geriatric witches and warlocks lounging around the pool with way too much skin displayed.

I'M MARISSA HALE, AND THAT'S HOW IT STARTED. That's how my brief vacation in Willow Hill, Florida, became more about work than a summer getaway. Well, also because Gran promised to hook me up with her outstanding stylist, who she claimed was practically a magician with hair repair.

It was bad enough Gran had to let me crash at

her condo under the scrutiny of a bunch of ancient witches eager for gossip that I will provide. I just couldn't bear to borrow more money from her, too, so I snagged a job at Night Moves. My good fortune was mainly because the bar was one cocktail server down after an employee, who was a vamp, got carried away with a customer. Apparently, the boss, Vlad, permits no blood sucking, blatant magic, or any other dangerous paranormal shenanigans on the premises. And they called this a paranormal night club?

So, when they fired the vamp, they hired me. Luckily, they were desperate, and they knew my gran. If they'd checked my less than stellar references, they might have hesitated.

Not that I'm not a skilled worker. It's that my charmed cocktails take practice to make perfect. I was told I might get a chance at the role of charmed cocktail mixologist after my probationary period. Although Vlad might have said that to make me stop asking about the position.

I should've listened to Gran and kept my cocktail attempts under wraps until I could prove I was an exceptional magical mixologist, but I wasn't sure I'd be in Florida that long, and thought I knew better. It took time for me to fit in anywhere—if ever. My personality was more sarcastic than sparkling, and after losing the last job, my lack of confidence was showing up in my charms.

And it was one of those charms that had me at the dumpster behind Night Moves. My cattail cocktail had just blown up, and I needed to take the volatile remnants outside before I caused more damage. I don't know what happened, but it seemed as if the ingredients had gotten mixed up or mislabeled, almost like someone intentionally messed with the spelling supplies I'd stashed under the bar.

I'd had a lot of mishaps in my time, but not a doozy quite like this one.

2

The club was empty—one good thing about being stuck on the early shift—and it gave me plenty of time to work on my charmed cocktails unobserved. Burton, the bartender Gran referred to, was more than a little odd, but he was fine with me practicing mixing drink potions. Well, he didn't really respond to my request. I took that as a yes. Thank the goddess for small favors.

I carried the sizzling, warped drink tray in front of me. A smoky residue rose from the center where a big, black patch was all that remained of the shot glass. I sucked in a breath and tried to hold it to avoid the overpowering stench reminiscent of burnt popcorn. I needed to get the club aired out before anyone else arrived. My current indigestion was most likely a delayed response from tasting the cattail cocktail before it blew. I could only hope my stomach wouldn't suffer the same fate.

I was almost to the dumpster when my shoe caught on a loose stone and I teetered forward. As I swung my free arm to maintain my balance, I gritted out, "Oh no."

My ankles wobbled in my new shoes, and my stomach rolled. Words flew from my mouth that could've mistakenly been interpreted as a spell. "Listen to me, feet, and don't be talking back to me, cattails cocktail."

When the tray shook, I clutched it tighter. The last of the burnt ingredients on the tray set off one last blast, tossing me into a pile of trash that softened my landing, but not my bruised ego.

"Broken broom sticks!" My tingling scalp confirmed that I'd have a new streak for this magical mistake. If my clientele realized the trouble I went through to create a new cocktail, perhaps I'd get a bigger tip now and then.

I ran my hand over my hair, wondering where the new dark streak would peek through. Thank the new moon that Gran had hooked me up with an appointment with Joe, a hairstylist at Supernatural Strands or Super Strands for short. Fortunately for Joe, and unfortunately for me, I never seemed to learn my lesson. No wonder I was always broke.

I lay in the pile of discarded trash while staring at that same blue sky Gran had raved about. Would I ever catch a break? "Thank the goddess, no one saw this embarrassment."

"Oh, but I did."

I pushed up on my elbows and looked around. "Who? Who's out here?"

A black cat peered around the corner of the dumpster. "Why, I am."

"What?" I rubbed my head and stared at the cat. He stared back with large, inquisitive golden eyes. "Did you just say something?"

"Of course I did. Did you lose your hearing when you fell? Or just your dignity?" The cat twitched his whiskers and narrowed his eyes. Then, as if a dam broke, his complaints poured out like verbal diarrhea: he'd been waiting outside forever, the human who usually fed him hadn't today, so it was now my responsibility, etc. He explained that after witnessing the mini explosion and my resulting fall, he had little faith I'd be able to keep him fed.

I was being insulted by a cat. A cat that could talk and understand me. Although he'd yet to stop talking, so I wasn't sure he was doing much on the listening part, much like most of the men in my life. The cat had further validated his maleness by sashaying too close to my face, giving me an up close and frightful view of his family jewels.

I laid my arm across my forehead and closed my eyes to wait until the world stopped spinning and random cats stopped talking. Had I hit my head harder than I thought? I'd previously tried, and failed, multiple spells to allow me to communicate with Mulder. I finally gave up before I injured my dog or myself.

When I opened my eyes, the cat was still there. In my face. Talking. "I see from your cheap name tag your name is Marissa. I'm not sure why humans have to put a tag on their shirt or on the collar of their animal family members to remember their names. Is your memory that bad?"

"I—"

"My name is Jasper." The cat held up a paw as if he would actually give me time to respond. "No tag needed. I'll remind you if you forget. Now, can you get me something better to eat than the slop dumped out here?"

I sat up, squeezed my eyes shut, then opened them again. My vision focused clearly on the cat, who continued to complain about the slim pickings around the dumpster. Perhaps it was a good thing the communication spell had never worked with Mulder.

Who'd have thought animals had so much to gripe about?

What I would've told Jasper, if he'd let me get a word out, was that the club drew many vampires who didn't eat and werewolves who ate just about anything. We were lucky to have much to toss out at all.

I held up a hand. "Stop. Ok, Jasper. I'm not sure how long this spell is going to last, if indeed it's a spell and not a curse or,"—I pinched my arm—"I'm not passed out and hallucinating. But if you'll stop talking, I'll see what I can do about getting you something to eat."

He cocked his head to the side. "Sounds good, human named Marissa. Let's go."

I smiled when he hopped on my lap. He was cute when he was quiet. "Mulder will love you."

I hoped I wasn't as wrong about that as I was about this being an easy summer job. Gran always said I went looking for trouble. Luckily, when I told Jasper I'd wake him once I found him something to eat, he curled up on my jacket in my locker and immediately fell asleep.

I headed toward the kitchen to search for food to sneak to the cat. No one was at the club yet, but other employees would arrive shortly. Although, for all I knew, the only thing anyone else might hear if he woke up and started complaining before I returned was meowing. The boss wouldn't permit having a cat in the club. While not in human form, even weres and shifters couldn't hang out here.

I shoved my face into the freezer to find something to defrost for Jasper while cooling my sweaty skin from the furnace of Florida heat. My plan backfired in a hurry when I came face to face with a frosty-looking corpse.

There were many things I might've expected to find in the extra freezer in the back room of the Night Moves kitchen, but a corpse wasn't anywhere on that list. This day was getting better and better.

I dropped the lid of the chest freezer and stepped back to stare at the bulky appliance. First a talking cat and now a corpse? Maybe I'd imagined the dead man tucked in with the frozen food. Perhaps, as previously considered, this was all a blackout dream, and I was actually lying unconscious in the parking lot.

I stepped forward and pulled on the lid a second time. A sucking sound caught my attention as the seal broke, and the gust of cool air bursting out had me tensing as if the freezer had come alive. I hesitated in case the corpse might rise from the frozen depths. I might be a witch, but I was more of a scaredy cat than Jasper.

As the cold fog dissipated, I swallowed and stepped forward to peer over the edge of the freezer. Yep. There was still a dead guy nestled in among the frozen fish and hamburger patties. A hand touched my shoulder and I let out a scream. I spun to face my assailant. "Burton! What are you doing? You nearly frightened me to death."

My coworker, Burton, peered over my shoulder. As usual, his black hair glistened with pomade. "Like that guy?"

Burton's tone was as flat as if he'd just announced the time and not commented on the corpse in the freezer. His emotions were few, if they existed at all. I knew he was something different from the moment I met him; I just hadn't figured out what yet.

I pressed my hand against my galloping heart. Now would've been a good time for me to be free of my own pesky emotions. So what if my feelings were often overabundant; I'd take that over being the sinister-looking, silent type, like Burton, even if it made him a good listener. He'd become my sounding board during my first month as I struggled to fit in. He, of all people, understood what it was like to be compared to everyone else and come up lacking.

The nice thing about having Burton as the closest thing to a best friend that Florida offered was that I didn't have to worry about hurting his non-existent feelings. He didn't give a bat's eye what anyone else thought. He was just Burton. Sure, it made him come across a little creepy to some, but his utter indifference was his best feature and something I aspired to have for myself. So far, I was failing in my quest.

I looked at my creepy coworker, unsure of how to break our silent standoff. For once, Burton knew exactly what to say. He cocked his head to the side, appearing more curious than concerned. "What happened to him?"

"How am I supposed to know?" We both peered into the freezer.

"Wait. I think I know him." I leaned forward far enough that my toes almost left the ground and tried to envision the corpse without the frosty coating. The thick chest curls peeking from the collar of his shirt and the seventies-style handlebar mustache confirmed it. "He lives in Gran's retirement community. His name is Henry." I grimaced at the memory of the pool. "He was wearing a lot less clothing the last time I saw him." It seemed Henry wouldn't be strutting any more of his stuff for the witches.

3

The unpleasant view of Henry strutting around in that little bathing suit would've been welcome over finding him defrosting as we held the freezer lid open. "I can't believe I just found Henry in the freezer."

"What did you find? Some old, expired meat?" Samantha sashayed into the storage room, which now felt cramped with the four of us, even if one of us was in the freezer and no longer sharing the same air. Not that Samantha needed much air as a vampire, or much space since she was tall and thin as a rail.

"You could say that, but it wouldn't be very considerate." I winced as soon as the comment left my lips. Some enjoyed a little sarcasm, but it was unlikely this was the best place to use such humor. What could I say? This was my first murder scene.

Samantha sped across the floor with her abnor-
mally fast vampire speed until she was hovering
between us. After a quick glimpse, she retreated as if
she wanted to put as much distance between herself
and the corpse—or Burton and me—as possible.

"What happened?" She narrowed her violet eyes
and ran her gaze over both of us as if we were emit-
ting clues. I withered like a guilty school child being
reprimanded, even though I'd done nothing wrong.
Burton didn't appear as if her comment, or the
corpse, affected him at all. I could only assume dead
bodies were a normal part of his week.

Finding my voice, I said, "Someone murdered
Henry," with as much flair as I'd seen on many of
those television crime shows Gran loved to watch.

"How do you know it's a murder?" Her attention
went right to Burton; her head shifted so quickly that
the hair in her blonde pixie cut swayed.

"Do you think he got into the freezer to take a
nap? It's not like he misjudged it for a casket." I
frowned, wondering if that would've made a differ-
ence to a vampire. Technically, they weren't really
alive, so would an air-tight freezer mean the end of
them? Probably a question for a better time.

"He's not a vampire." She narrowed her gaze. "You
called him Henry. So, you knew him?" Her neck
swiveled from Henry to Burton to me as she sniffed

the air like a bloodhound on a scent before she said, "I smell magic."

I took another look at Henry and sure enough, his clothing had spelling residue burnt into it. The big, white collar, made popular in the seventies, had a glittery glow with black magic soot speckling it.

When I returned my focus to Samantha, she was staring at my hair, obviously homing in on the new streak. "Wait. I—"

"You two better stay right there. I'm going to get Vlad," she said, backing away and pointing from Burton to me as if Henry might mistake her comment for him. A gust of air whooshed by as she left the room with lightning speed.

"What's that supposed to mean? Just because I barely knew Henry, and because I'm a witch, doesn't mean I did anything wrong. I found him—that's it!" I hated feeling like I had to defend myself for something I didn't do, even though she'd already left the room.

I resisted touching my hair. When I'd returned inside with Jasper, a glance to the mirrors behind the bar had confirmed what I'd suspected: I'd earned a new dark streak from the blown up cocktail incident in the parking lot. The twist I'd fashioned my hair into could only conceal so much.

If I admitted the truth behind the streak, that I

was charming cocktails without permission, I'd likely lose my job. Charming cocktails showed off the best of my magic talents. Well, pretty much my only talent. If I could show Vlad how customers grew to love my specialty drinks, I'm sure he'd overlook my disregard for the probationary period. My preference was to ask for an apology later rather than permission first.

If Samantha didn't get me fired. She had it in for me from the start. It wasn't my fault that the vamp I replaced was her friend. Then, I asked about her new boyfriend one time, not realizing he was the husband of one regular customer. With a strict rule about not messing around with the married clientele, Vlad wasn't happy about that news at all, and my harmless observation had gotten her written up. I wouldn't put it past her to seek revenge, but murder seemed pretty harsh, especially killing an old, harmless warlock like Henry.

But Samantha was a vampire, and a reckless one —if the rumors were true. Maybe she'd jumped Henry for a blood cocktail last night and then stashed him in the freezer. She knew I had the early shift today. She could've planted the magic residue on Henry to misdirect the blame on me. I peered closer at Henry. He'd have a bite mark somewhere on him if his death was because of a vampire, but they could conceal a bite on all parts of the body. Literally, on any part...

I cringed at the thought of examining his body for a bite mark and leaned even farther back from the freezer. Maybe it was best to leave the examination to the police. The creaking of the door had me spinning around, but it was just Burton attempting a stealthy exit from the room.

"Where are you going? Samantha said to wait," I said. She wasn't my supervisor, even though she pretended she was, but I was trying my best to stay in Vlad's good graces, and that stick-skinny vampire was a huge suck up. Plus, it seemed wrong to leave Henry alone in the freezer, and me alone with a dead body. "You can't go. Isn't that like leaving the scene of the crime?"

"But I didn't find him. You did," he said and then smoothed his hand down his impeccable dark purple pinstriped suit. "I have to tend bar."

I sighed. Burton had a good work ethic, but there was no reasoning with him. He had his routines and didn't veer from them. I swear if the place burst into flames, he would extinguish a spot small enough to continue manning the bar. "Can't that wait?"

Burton crossed his arms and looked down at me. He wasn't much taller, but he made up for it with his impassive expression that gave the appearance of being completely empty inside and not giving a hoot if you joined in the ranks of the deceased. "Do you want to contend with one dead body? Or a club full of angry paranormals waiting for their drinks?"

I was pretty sure he meant Henry when he referred to the dead body, although others might have taken Burton's comments as a veiled threat. And I also knew there was one nasty witch who didn't like to wait on their beverage of choice. I don't know what I did to earn gin-and-juice Gloria's dislike, but that bitter witch cut me to the core with insults. I'd hate to see what she could do if she got upset enough to retaliate with magic. "You have a point. Henry isn't going anywhere." I closed the freezer and followed Burton out.

A quick check on Jasper confirmed he was still asleep; exhaustion must've overwhelmed the poor kitty. It was a good thing he was napping, because if the noise filtering to the back was any sign, the club was rapidly filling up. After a quick check in with the boss and Samantha, Vlad insisted we take care of the customers while he determined the next steps for the body.

Many supernatural clientele were preening and prancing around the club. Okay, maybe not all of them were preening and prancing, but the atmosphere sure felt weird. How could the world just keep going as normal with Henry chilling in our freezer as if he'd simply settled in for a nap?

You'd think that dealing with a dead body would be more of a common occurrence for a bunch of paranormals, but apparently murdering and sticking a warlock in a freezer differed from bleeding them out or other possible unnatural fates normals suffered in present company. Those unsavory outcomes seemed to fall into more of "vampires will be vampires" or "paranormals will be paranormal" view around here. The attitude must've come from living in a small town where everyone knew about everyone... if they were paranormal.

It did not exactly upset Vlad about Henry. He was more troubled that this might disrupt tonight's service. As the club got busier, no one seemed to know how to deal with the corpse while continuing business as usual. Either reduce our available menu options or dig around the body for the frozen food? Finally, someone had the idea of donating the food to a local shelter for wayward werewolves. After Henry was no longer using the frozen meat patties as a mattress, of course.

I didn't really know him all that well, but continuing on with the day as if nothing happened felt rather heartless. I said as much to Burton, but he didn't respond, although I'd like to think the situation upset him. He didn't seem to care strongly enough about anything to seek revenge or hate. For him, everything and everyone was just business.

He was the only supe I knew with this attitude. Or I should say, the only one I knew and liked. The one other person I knew with a similar devil-may-care attitude was Gloria, a witch that made my every day a living nightmare with her rude comments. She wore her indiscretions with pride in a veil of blacker than coal hair that confirmed she'd done more than her share of horrid spells. Which confirmed she might be hateful enough to seek revenge for the most minor indiscretion.

I leaned against the bar as Burton filled my tray with another round of drinks. Normals—a never-ending supply of tourists passing through, snowbirds flocking to escape the winter, and newbies who'd just retired—disappeared a lot around this area, but Henry wasn't a normal. Henry was one of our own and he hadn't disappeared. Surely, the other staff should be more concerned? Part of me wondered if the lack of concern was because he was a warlock. Witches and warlocks made up the smallest group of paranormals in town.

I couldn't get Henry out of my mind. Even for a warlock, he might've been old, but I suspected foul play. Who would crawl into a freezer to commit suicide? Heck, I wasn't sure at Henry's age that he could manage that on its own.

That magic residue had to mean something, but I wasn't about to point that out as the only witch here for the start of the shift who'd also found Henry's body. The same witch who was sporting a new spelling streak in her hair. Of course, this was all coincidence, but I was kidding myself to think everyone would believe that.

❧ 4 ❧

Vlad raised a thin black brow, as if my suggestion of notifying the police was absurd. "Around these parts, paranormals take care of their own and avoid involving the mortal police until necessary. I want to keep Henry's death close to the vest until I get to the bottom of things."

I nodded and hustled away to deliver Gloria's drink, fearing the bottom was where I might end up if the consensus landed on the new witch playing a part in Henry's death.

"What did you do to earn that?" Gloria smiled smugly.

I pretended I didn't notice her intense focus on my hair, or understand what she implied, and stated the obvious. "Here's your drink." She'd be the last person I'd tell about Jasper, even if it would explain my magical blunder.

A quick check on Jasper confirms he's still asleep. Exhaustion must have overwhelmed the poor kitty, so I let him sleep rather than wake him for the tuna I'd found in the back of the cupboard. I'd give him the treat later.

I resist the temptation to pull Jasper out of my locker and confess to everyone that the new dark streak in my hair was from a misspell that enabled me to talk to a cat. Because there was a good chance no one else could understand his meows, this idea would likely only make me look irrational. On second thought, it might enable me to use an insanity plea if I end up unjustly charged.

So far, the only suspects I'd identified included that suck up Samantha and grating on my last nerve, Gloria, who'd been dying to get into Gran's retirement community. I wouldn't put it past her to make her own vacancy in the Willow Hill Witch condominiums by killing off one resident.

I leaned over the bar to whisper to Burton, "Everyone thinks we have something to do with Henry's death."

Burton shrugged and continued pouring drinks.

I didn't think he had anything to do with the murder, but I needed to confirm my assumption, which meant keeping my eye on him. The concept proved challenging when I couldn't find him several times during the shift. Odd, considering he was usually behind the bar unless the occasional need to bounce someone who got too rowdy popped up. For Burton, that typically only required an extended look and the offender would leave quickly. His lengthy absences tonight had me wondering where he'd been hiding and it made him look guilty—of what, I wasn't sure.

But each time, as soon as I fretted, there he was again, standing in his usual spot. When I questioned him about his whereabouts, he raised a brow oddly that makes me hesitate to challenge him and replied that he never left.

After I thought back, I realized there had been other nights when I couldn't find him. I'd dismissed his absence because I was busy with customers or caught up in my own priorities.

I rarely paid him much attention when I was working, but it makes me feel guilty to admit—even if only to myself—that he's a means to an end. We make a great team because he's almost intuitive, as though he knows exactly what I want before I've asked. Tonight has shown me I may have been taking him for granted.

I glanced toward the bar from where I stand at

the back of the room. Burton is there, but he's not serving drinks or standing in his usual cement statue pose. I frown. What is he up to? He's acting weirder than usual.

When the band finally starts, people rush to the dance floor and I move toward the wall to avoid spilling the tray of drinks or getting crushed in the mass of bodies. I'm careful to avoid the groups starting up their lackluster, alcohol-infused dance moves.

Burton backs away from the bar top until he's directly in front of the shelves of liquor. After a stealthy glance from one side to the other, he raises his hand above his head to touch the weird, ugly statue I'd complained about from day one and then— poof!—he disappeared.

What the? Did I blink? Where the hell did he go?

I continued to struggle as I pushed my way through the throng of people and got sidetracked along the way by several customers wanting to place drink orders who had no clue I was on a mission to discover where the heck Burton snuck off to. If he had a secret hiding place to escape the masses of people and the deafening volume, he'd better share it with me.

By the time I got to the bar, he was standing

there like he'd never left. He studied my exasperated face with a curious expression of his own.

I set my drink tray on the bar. "Where did you go?"

He glanced around at his obvious presence as if I'd suddenly become feeble-minded. "Here."

"No, you weren't here a few minutes ago. I—"

I was going to call him on it and insist that I saw him disappear, but after noting the tension lining his jaw and the way he tightened the muscles there just a tad, I knew he was lying.

If I pressed him about it now, I'd never find out where he went. Based on tonight's events and because of my insatiable curiosity, I simply had to know where he'd gone. I worked with Burton, but knew very little about him. He did his job, listened more than he spoke, and refused to share any personal details. This mystery was a chance to look a little deeper beneath his expressionless facade.

"Nothing." I forced a chuckle. "The band probably distracted me. They're really pulling them in tonight, huh? That should make Vlad happy." I chatted on to distract him from realizing what I might, or might not, have seen.

Once I'd decided upon Operation Burton, I wouldn't stop. I'd either be able to clear his name or confirm what everyone else already suspected.

Keeping most of my focus on the bar and Burton while I worked wasn't all that challenging—except for when I almost dumped a drink on one customer, and placed a glass on another's hand instead of the table. To erase their scowl, I'd laughed it off as if I'd intended to do that.

As the crowd got larger and rowdier, I kept as close to the bar as possible. When Burton started his stealthy retreat to the rear of the bar, I moved in with a long list of drink orders. He wasn't starting with the disappearing act right when I needed his help. Not this time.

But he was gone when I arrived. Oh, heck to the no.

My tray landed on the bar with a clatter and I rushed behind the counter, standing in the same place where I'd last seen him. Nothing happened. After looking around, my gaze settled on the only thing that didn't really belong in this place, but that Burton had completely ignored my requests to get rid of. I raised onto my toes and craned my hand over my head and struggled to touch the ugly monstrosity of a statue. Once I felt the cold stone, I waited, and... nothing.

This position left me looking like I was doing a weird yoga stretch and allowed ogling from a few men who'd sidled up to the bar to find me with my arm raised, boobs thrust forward, and my stomach exposed to display my bellybutton ring.

"Cauldrons!" I left my odd post and went to serve the leering customers. Once I got their orders, I turned and bumped directly into Burton. Stealth mode was over. I needed answers if I had any hope of eliminating him as a suspect. "Where did you go? I saw you touch the thingy up there and then you disappeared. I tried to follow you, but I couldn't. Why? I did the same thing you did." I blathered on, eager to rid myself of the charade of pretending I didn't know something was going on.

He studied me for a long beat. "Nowhere."

"It wasn't nowhere. Come on, you can tell me. I won't share your secret hiding place with anyone else. I just want to check it out. Maybe I could use it occasionally when I need a breather." Plus, I really wanted to know one of his secrets. We all have them, and most people can't keep secrets for long, but Burton was obviously an exception. He knew plenty, assuming he actually listened all the times I spilled my guts about my latest blunders. Sharing them with him felt like putting them in a vault because he told no one anything.

"You can tell me. I tell you tons of my secrets." My sweet smile faltered when he maintained his expressionless, unblinking stare. I raised my hand and extended all five fingers. "Fine, then I'll keep stalking you. My distraction will cause my customers to suffer." I ticked off a finger. "Vlad will get mad and we'll both have to hear about it." Another finger lowered.

I paused. Still nothing.

I threw up both hands. "Doesn't it seem kind of silly not to tell me? It would save a lot of time and frustration for both of us." I didn't think he really cared about any of these things. I was counting on him telling me to get me to stop talking and leave him alone.

"Don't follow me." He narrowed his gaze.

I paused again, uncertain if this was a threat. His tone was consistent, as usual. "So, you're admitting you're sneaking off to a secret place? Tell me I'm right. Show me the place you're going once, and I swear I'll leave you alone. Otherwise, I'll keep trying to pull on that weird statue until it lets me in."

"It won't let you in, ever, and besides, it's not safe for you." His voice rose a little.

This was one of the longest sentences Burton had ever said to me, and I didn't particularly care for how he pointed out that I, specifically, wouldn't be allowed into his secret clubhouse. "But if I went with you, I'd be safe. Wouldn't I?" I reached for his hand. "You know everything about me. We're friends, aren't we? Shouldn't you share a little about yourself?"

I had to know something about him, anything, to validate that we were the friends I thought we were despite our odd relationship that tested the boundaries and usual criteria for most friendships. Despite him challenging all the familiar norms, I considered him a friend.

He remained silent, staring at me with an even more serious expression than he usually wore—which I hadn't realized was possible until now. Could it be that he was concerned about me?

I smiled. "What in the world wouldn't be safe about a hidey-hole in Night Moves?" I hoped he didn't point out that the corpse in the freezer might challenge my claim about the safety of the club.

The muscle in his jaw twitched. I was wearing him down. "Why isn't it safe? Is it because I'm a woman? Or a witch? Seriously, Burton, you know I can take care of myself."

"Because you're not a demon." He said the words as if they were the most obvious reason.

"Obviously. But neither are you—"

My mouth gaped long enough to make me feel ridiculous when I realized it was hanging open. "But you... you can't... they don't..."

As the protests tumbled from my lips, more

puzzle pieces fell into place. Burton was different, but he was just Burton. Plus, demons didn't walk the earth, did they? If he was a demon, where were his horns and spiked tail? Why hadn't he mutilated me and others long ago? The most disturbing thought was, why did he and I get along so well? That had to mean something. But I said nothing.

5

W hat do you say to a friend who reveals that they consider the bowels of hell their home? Someone who sought souls to serve with a piece of warm, crusty bread—or at least that's how I envisioned it. But instead of asking any of these outrageous questions, I asked an equally stupid question. After all, I felt like I had to say something rather than continue with our silent stare off bound to end with his piercing stare setting me on fire. "Is that why you chose Florida, because it's so hot? It reminds you of home?"

My laugh felt forced and Burton didn't join in. Not that he ever did. I'd never seen him laugh, and that should've been my first clue. What did demons find funny? Watching people burn on a fiery spit?

A demon? Just when I thought I'd heard it all, I learned I worked alongside a demon. Who knew? Not me, but I wondered if anyone else did. This could confirm his responsibility for Henry's death, and put one more nail in Burton's coffin... or, more like, one more log on his hellfire. Perhaps Henry had stumbled onto his secret and Burton had shoved him in the freezer to cool him off after making him burst into flame with a glance—or whatever it was demons did.

Nah. Demon or not, I couldn't see Burton doing anything like that, but maybe I was naïve. The sad part was that I liked him a lot better than many of my customers and coworkers. "A demon? But you're so nice."

My words fell flat once I realized what I considered nice. Being a good listener with a dead-flat expression, intimidating rambunctious customers, and an air of creepy mystery were all potential traits of a demon. Since I'd never met one before, that I knew of, I didn't even know if Burton was a good representation of his demon brethren.

What was the world coming to? And where in the world—or should I say, out of, or below, this world—was Burton disappearing to? Perhaps this explained why there were so many supernatural species frequenting Night Moves. Maybe there was more going on—or under—than I realized. I had a lot of questions, but I was sure Burton wouldn't agree to an interrogation about his top-secret hell retreat. But what was he doing down there? I couldn't drop this. Without my help, he was looking guiltier than most.

Lucky for me, Burton's never-ending patience left him waiting with his silent stare as all these possibilities ran through my mind.

"Why do you keep disappearing? If I can't go with you, can you at least tell me what you're doing? You have enough dirt on me to bury at least five vamps and what's left of my lackluster reputation since I've been babbling all my blunders to you." I paused. What could Burton do with my confessions of misdeeds and what some might consider unladylike behavior, even for a witch? Was he compiling a list of my indiscretions to secure me a hot seat in the afterworld's underbelly?

"You haven't been sharing what I've... er, what I've told you, have you?" I twisted my hands together, unable to even fathom the long list of indiscretions I'd accumulated with my wayward, witchy ways. It was a little late for me to turn over a new leaf. Besides, any demon wouldn't have to work hard to gather info on wrongdoings when this wonky witch served up her sins on a silver platter with a shot of tequila. Which is exactly what I could use right about now.

"No. I'm just doing my job." He glanced at the drink orders and began mixing them with efficient, expert grace.

I swallowed. Did he mean his job for Night Moves, or whatever potential other job he might have as a demon? For a second time, I longed for that shot of tequila before I broached this subject. Even if I didn't want to know the answer, I needed more information. "Henry?"

"Who?" His brows lowered in confusion as he set down the bottle of vodka.

"The guy we found in the freezer."

He shook his head. "I had nothing to do with him."

I exhaled.

Dang it. And what was his demon job? Were the snazzy suits part of the dress code, or was that just his preference? Did they make deals for the devil or sell souls? As a demon, he must have been up to more than tending bar and bouncing. Some nights, work felt like hell itself, but I'd never thought that might actually be our physical location. I frowned, contemplating what Burton's job might entail.

He tensed and paused, his cocktail shaking. The ice settled, and the silence hung heavy between us. His eyes locked with mine. "Whatever you're thinking, you're right." He turned and continued with his task of straining the chilled cocktail into the martini glasses. Once the drinks were complete, he turned and carried them down to the other end of the bar.

Did he read my mind? Or was I just that transparent? Ava always said my thoughts displayed on my face, but she was my twin, so we had that connection.

Souls? Devil deals? This would be a good time for Burton to talk more and listen less. Otherwise, I'd continue to seal my fate. I'd already established that I didn't do well in the heat. If I had to spend an eternity festering away in an underground sauna, I'd never last, and my hair would frizz to high heaven.

Even if he killed Henry, Burton operated on logic. I took another look at Burton, where he was methodically mixing drinks. Would he consider the freezer a good place to tuck a corpse so it didn't hamper business? Maybe. But when he came upon me peering at Henry in the freezer, he probably would've just said that he needed killing, and leave it at that.

I needed to get clues into Henry's murder to clear my name and Burton's.

I intended to approach Burton to question him about his whereabouts, but lost my nerve. Was my judgement clouded by my dislike of Samantha and Gloria? Both seemed like better suspects, yet all the gossip I heard pointed to the fact that no one considered either of them.

Vlad said a guy would come around to help sort out this mess. I didn't trust the way his gaze lingered on me when he said the word mess. Even if I proved to be an exceptional charmed cocktail mixologist, if Vlad thought I was a murderer, he'd fire me.

I needed to get Jasper, go home, and talk to Gran. She'd know what to do. She knew the folks around here. Gran might be a little—or a lot—eccentric, speak when she really should filter what she says, and dress in attire more suitable for someone thirty years her junior, but she's a well-respected witch. Surely, that would count for something.

And she knew Henry. I sighed and glanced at the clock as my shift wound down. Someone had to tell Gran that Henry was dead. Not just dead— murdered. A conversation like that was probably better done in person rather than a text or phone call. This news would have to wait until I got home.

The guy finally showed up to review the crime scene. If you could call it that.

"He barely even looked at Henry and he's eating up everything Samantha's telling him." I complained to Burton as I imagined the accusations the vengeful vamp was probably making about me while she leaned in to the were. I thought he'd be immune to her vamp charms. Apparently not.

He started heading my way while keeping a wary gaze on Burton. It was easy to see why Burton would be the prime suspect. Even if he didn't know his true job—which I deduced was to guard the gates of the Underworld—my demon buddy didn't look like the friendliest fella. His demeanor made him a great bouncer, but not so great as a people-person.

I cleared my throat, preparing to make my statement, but the guy veered into Vlad's office. A few moments later, Vlad motioned me over.

"Marissa, I think you should get Burton's statement," Vlad said.

"What? Why me?" Not even the bravest of paranormals would directly accuse Burton of murdering Henry.

"Because you have some kind of awkward rapport with him, and the least seniority. Don't forget, you found the body." Vlad walked away, ending the conversation.

How could I forget? That alone had me firmly in line for runner-up on the suspect list. It also became obvious that I was the only one who really cared about getting justice for Henry. My motivation to help might have been pure, but asking me to question a demon, friend or not, was outside of my pay grade. That, and I really didn't want to find out that Burton wasn't actually a good guy.

It was time to pack up my talking cat and bring in some outside magical help: Gran.

6

"So you're saying you found Henry dead in the freezer at Night Moves?" Gran leaned back in her threadbare recliner until her bright blue painted toenails came into view and the multi-colored afghan hanging over the back of the chair puddled on the floor. She took a thoughtful sip of her margarita and closed her eyes. "Girl, you make a darn good cocktail, if I say so myself. Although I take some credit for the talent behind those crafty charmed beverages. You must've inherited those skills from me."

I raised a brow. Surely, she wouldn't want to take credit for the hot mess that my cocktails had gotten me into lately. Although, I hadn't shared the story about Jasper the talking cat yet. When I'd retrieved him from my locker, he complained that I'd woke him from his slumber, but as soon as he woke up, he'd realized I still hadn't brought him any food. To appease him, I'd packed him in my shoulder bag along with a customer's leftover swordfish.

It would take forever to get the fishy smell out of my bag and even longer for my ears to stop ringing from his complaints that I'd given him leftovers instead of his own personal dinner. Maybe I was wrong to assume he would've preferred the swordfish over the old can of tuna I'd found. Frankly, he was lucky I remembered to get his food at all after spending the shift trying to clear my name and identify potential murder suspects. His endless yammering confirmed I could still understand him, an ability I regretted on the long walk home.

My gaze shifted to my bedroom where I'd stashed the persnickety feline, despite his lengthy protests, until I could tell Gran about Henry.

I realize everyone grieves differently, but her nonchalant behavior was a little unusual. Gran was never afraid to show her emotions; they usually came out in one big eruption, whether anger, sadness, or happiness, before she simply moved on. Her ability to handle stress by bottling nothing up was probably what kept her living such a carefree life.

"Gran. This was Henry," I repeated and then braced myself for the onslaught of emotions.

She waved me off and looked toward the window to study the bird feeder hanging outside. It was currently vacant of birds, although that might've been because of a particular squirrel who continually emptied the contents as quickly as Gran could fill it. "I heard you the first time. Henry is dead. At my age, people die all the time."

I leaned forward, resting my elbows on my knees to gain her full attention and drive my point home. "But someone murdered him. His death isn't really the same thing."

"That's true." She nodded and rubbed her chin thoughtfully. "Murder is different. I knew it would be nice to have you around. It gets boring here, but now you can bring me all the new gossip, even if you are a little late with your delivery."

I'd expected more of a reaction to the news. Henry was well known in the retirement community. Aside from his outrageous behavior and unforgettable attire, the females outnumbered the males. Many ladies had been vying for his attention since I'd been here.

"You seem to take his murder pretty well." I frowned, wondering if she was in shock. "Wait. What do you mean I'm late?"

"You're about the sixth person to tell me about, Henry. Then there's the Willow Words." She picked up a thin newsletter and shook it. "But we never know if Fran gets any story right, since she's always in such a rush to publish the scoop first. Heck, Fran has reported more than one person dead who's only been away visiting family. She's quick to jump the gun."

"The willow what?"

"Our condo newsletter, of course." Gran tossed it to me.

The headline for the retirement home newsletter read, "Henry Miller Found Dead in Club Freezer by Esther's granddaughter." The article below it discussed how Henry ending up in the freezer was ironic since his favorite phrases included some version of hell freezing over. There were several pictures of Henry with Fred and other residents of the retirement condos.

I glanced at Gran. She raised her brows as she observed me. I returned my attention to the paper. If the lighthearted discussion of Henry's death wasn't disturbing enough, they'd also featured an unflattering photo of me walking to work in my Night Moves uniform. My wilted hair under the hot Florida heat and the sheen of sweat covering my face and arms were clearly visible.

When my eyes landed back on Gran, aka Esther, I was speechless for one of the few times in my life. The only thing I could sputter out was, "How?"

She smiled as though she read my mind that it wasn't Henry's death I was referring to. Knowing Gran, mind reading was entirely possible. "Marissa, dear, you'll need to get used to everyone knowing absolutely everything about everyone here. We're retired and have little else to do except live vicariously through other people. That's the fun of retirement."

I cringed at the reminder that I was now bunking in a retirement community. One that apparently took secret, unsolicited, unflattering photos of me. At least they took this one before I'd gained the new black streak. I'm sure my magical mishaps would provide Fran with plenty of additional fodder for a plethora of stories. I looked at the newsletter again to locate the byline. "Who is Fran Stokes, and why is she taking pictures of me?"

Gran waved me off. "Oh, stop fussing. Fran lives here, of course, and I'm sure she has a stockpile of photos of everyone. She's always looking for the next scoop, so she likes to have photos ready just in case. With you here, well, I'm sure she thought you'd be in the paper, eventually."

Gran threw her head back with a laugh that shook her belly. "But I bet she was counting on one of those lifestyle pieces about who you are and what your life was like before Willow Hill. Not that there aren't a lot of juicy details in that story, but now with a murder, she's bound to be circling you for more of that breaking news. This is the biggest story since Fred went streaking after he lost a bet to Henry. Fran really regretted not getting a photo of that. She could have probably sold it to the highest bidder."

Her smile faded when she mentioned Henry. She looked down, suddenly interested in the small tear on the arm of her chair. Perhaps reality was settling in. I couldn't imagine losing so many friends or family over the years. Maybe her lighthearted attitude was her way of dealing with loss. She returned her focus to me. "What happened to your hair? Didn't Joe fix it at the salon?"

"Well..."

Gran sighed. "What did you do now? I told you it was a bad idea to experiment with those charmed cocktails at the club." She took another sip of her magical margarita. "Not that you aren't darn good at them, but everyone isn't as receptive to new things, or they might not have the stomach to handle the ingredients." She patted her own barrel-like belly.

"About that..." Maybe now was a good time to bring up Jasper. I could only hope that my new ability to converse with him didn't end up as the next story in the paper. I might have more quirks than most, but no need to let my freak flag out to fly fully.

Gran sat up straighter in her chair and her eyes brightened. "Supposedly, Henry was asking around for something he couldn't get with a spell. What's the name of that big bartender again? Could Henry have gotten on his nasty side?"

"Burton," I said. After a brief hesitation, I realized I had to tell someone. "He's a demon."

Her eyes widened. "A what? A demon?"

I nodded. Was a murder, a demon, and a talking cat too much to spring on her all at once?

Nope.

She leaned forward with a glimmer of excitement in her eyes. "I never considered demons might lurk among us. Did you see someone sign away their soul? Is that how you found out the truth?"

"No," I said. The old witch lived for this drama.

"Please don't tell me that's why you consider him a friend. You've rallied for some underdogs in the past, but sweetie, a demon can handle himself. Plus, he murdered Henry," Gran said.

"I don't think it was Burton."

Gran grunted her disagreement. She had mentioned more than once that I didn't have the best judgment. She knew me better than most, but still wouldn't give up her hope that I'd turn over a new leaf and consider more appropriate friends. Friends who didn't hail from hell and sign up new prospects like opening a checking account, with their soul as the deposit.

"Well, if you think so, but I wouldn't be so quick to rule a demon out from the list of suspects," she said with a nod.

Henry's interest in something magic couldn't provide wouldn't keep Burton off the suspect list. Burton provided many things. I'd just never realized what the price was for his services, and revealing his clients was probably breaking some kind of demon code of ethics. "Besides, there was spelling residue on Henry," I said.

Gran scowled. "Someone could plant that. The vamps and wolves have always had it out for us witches. Did they examine Henry thoroughly?"

"That's doubtful. I'm not sure what the usual protocol is for a murder, but they seemed more worried about him blocking the food." I winced when I said it. "How's Fred holding up?"

Gran shrugged. "Holed up in his condo. I stopped by, but he didn't answer the door. The poor guy is distraught. Can't say I blame him. Someone killed his best friend."

"Shouldn't we notify the police? Vlad brought in some guy who assumed it was Burton." I twisted a stray strand of my hair around my finger. "Or a witch."

"Land's sake, of course they wouldn't bring in the local police. They're mortal here. But that werewolf they use at the club for these sorts of fixes is always looking for a simple solution. Most vampires and werewolves stick together." She rolled her eyes. "They think they're higher ranking paranormals than the rest of us. We need to get our fella on it first, and then he can communicate with the police."

"Our fella?" It appeared the witches retirement village had its own little community, complete with all the amenities one could ask for. "Who's 'our fella'?"

7

"James Stone's the name."

I almost flew out of my chair when the raspy voice came from behind me and ended with a harsh cough. For a moment, I thought I'd heard a ghost. Heck, James Stone looked fairly spectral upon further inspection. His pink eyes, skin paler than mine, and light-colored clothing made him practically invisible.

Mulder took one look at him and retreated to the kitchen, forgoing his usual welcome of hopping about.

James's appearance gave the impression he was older than dirt. There was barely a hair left clinging to his scalp, despite an excess of hair sprouting from his white eyebrows. It was as if his eyebrows were trying to lower the expectation of his scalp to produce adequate coverage. The casual flowered button-down beach shirt hung untucked, and he wore khakis rolled up to display bony ankles. His attire, complete with flip-flops, didn't portray my image of a detective.

Gran interrupted my gawking to confirm that James was actually standing there and not an appari-tion. "For goddess' sake, Marissa. Quit gaping. Haven't you ever seen a person cursed to be pale as a ghost? They walk the earth while appearing like they've already left this world."

"Um, sorry." A response didn't seem necessary to confirm that obviously I had not, in fact, seen someone cursed in that manner. James Stone was just one more unusual thing on this unusual day. I stood and extended my hand. Part of me wondered if his hand would pass right through mine, like I envisioned a ghost's hand might. "Hi, I'm Marissa."

He ignored the gesture. Instead, he kept his hands in his pockets and stared at me while he rocked back and forth from his heels to his toes. "I know who you are. Everyone does," he said.

I glanced at the newsletter. "Of course you do."

"Your grandmother called me," he said and then sat on the couch and pulled out a small tablet and pencil. When he looked at me, his gaze settled briefly on the dark streak in my hair. I hadn't thought I'd need to conceal it in the comfort of my home—well, Gran's home.

He licked the tip of the pencil and then scribbled something in his notebook. I leaned forward from my chair but couldn't see what he was writing. Most likely something like how the streak in my hair elevated me to his number one suspect.

I settled back against one of the fringed pillows. This guy was Henry's best bet?

If I was honest with myself, it was likely the club would look for a scapegoat, and if it wasn't Burton, it would be me. Even worse, that meant a murderer would still be on the loose.

The elderly investigator seemed content to sit and scribble on that darn tablet, letting the silence stretch on. I wasn't as content. "Are you like a private investigator or something?"

He met Gran's gaze and then returned his attention to me. "Yeah, or something."

I waited, but it didn't sound like I was going to get any more explanation.

"You work at the club and were there at the time of the murder." He made the statement while keeping his expression blank.

If he thought he could intimidate me with a hard stare, he didn't know who he was up against. He couldn't compete with the likes of Burton. "After the murder." I pointed at his tablet. "I want to set the record straight." And I'd always wanted to say that last line.

"Sure. After." He scribbled something on the tablet again. "Tell me who you think might be a likely suspect at the club."

"Well, if it happened at the club. That's making an assumption, isn't it?" I looked from Gran to James.

He frowned and paused his incessant scribbling. "What do you mean by that?"

"The club wasn't open. The murder had to have happened the night before, and I doubt Henry was there that late," I said.

"That's true." Gran nodded vigorously enough to get her large hoop earrings swaying. "The part about Henry being there the night before. That club is open late. I mean, it's open way past nine o'clock."

James looked at me. "What time does the club close?"

I pursed my lips in concentration. "Usually last call is around two o'clock, but sometimes there are private vampire parties that are there until four or five a.m."

James and Gran locked gazes and then returned their attention to me before he spoke. "So you're saying it's open well past ten p.m.?"

"Yes. Aren't most night clubs?" This line of questioning seemed like a waste of time.

He shrugged. "Maybe. I wouldn't know. Once you get to a certain age, your priorities change. Getting to bed as early so you can get up as early as possible becomes much more standard. Not by choice, necessarily. It just happens as a natural part of aging. So, you're right. It's unlikely Henry was at the club so late. Therefore, it must've happened in the morning when you were there... alone."

"That's not what I meant," I said. "I meant someone could've killed Henry elsewhere and then put him into the club freezer."

James drew his brows down. "Why would the killer do that?"

I tossed my hands up. "I don't know. Isn't that what you're supposed to find out?"

He shrugged. "Maybe." He took more notes. "Tell me the suspect list again."

"I didn't tell you anyone yet."

He raised a brow. "That's what I said."

I looked from him to Gran, but she didn't meet my gaze. Had she hired someone whose memory was already faltering with age? It didn't happen often with witches, but from the spell this dude had already endured, anything was possible.

The odd investigator was still staring at me with

his unnerving pink eyes, so I named Samantha, Gloria, and then after hesitating, I added Burton.

Gran brightened. "He's a—"

I cut her off with a sharp look. It wouldn't help the investigation for Gran to push this guy to jump to conclusions with the rest of the club.

James looked at her. "He's what?"

She pursed her lips as if this new gossip was difficult to maintain. "An odd fella."

I nodded and then included a few details about Vlad and the other employees. If I was guilty until proven innocent, everyone else should be too.

One thing was abundantly clear: I was the only witch who worked there most of the time.

He stood. "Okay. I got what I need to get started."

"Wait. What are you going to do?" He had done little of anything except write information I already knew. Had he made his mind up about my or Burton's guilt already?

"What do you think? Detective stuff." And with that parting comment, he walked out the door.

I looked at Gran after he'd left. "Do you really think he's going to figure anything out?"

"No, not really. But he offered. At our age, we want to feel useful. I couldn't turn him down. Especially with all he's been through with that unbreakable curse. He's already a dead man walking, and he's still alive. It freaks people out and hasn't helped him find work. He has to limit his time in the sun, and can't take much work in the evenings because the vamps don't favor witches honing in on their preferred hours."

I slumped in the chair, feeling the weight of responsibility settle on my shoulders. "Is anyone else looking for Henry's killer?"

"Marissa, my dear, there comes a time when you realize you have to help yourself. When you want something done right, whether it's creating one of your charmed cocktails or solving a murder, you do it yourself," Gran said with a smile.

Gran's comment didn't exactly assure me, since I wasn't doing that great at either so far. "You're right. Henry deserves justice. If Vlad will not get it for him, I will."

A high-pitched squeaking sound startled me and I spun around, wondering what would be next on this ultra-bizarre day. "Jasper, is that you?" Jasper's laughter would sound like one of Mulder's squeaky toys. His amusement and obvious lack of faith in my ability to solve the murder didn't boost my confidence.

Jasper strutted down the hall with his tail held high, acting as if he owned the place. Because

Mulder had little to no interest in anything that wasn't food, it had been easy to smuggle the cat in without my favorite pup noticing. However, the skittering of claws across the kitchen floor announced that Mulder had now spotted the furry intruder, or that he thought the squeaky laugh was one of his toys. He locked his bulbous eyes on the cat. Mulder's mouth hung open and his tongue lolled out as he let out little excited huffs that were his version of barking.

After a quick assessment of the scene, Mulder raced full speed through the living room, likely intent on tackling Jasper. I jumped from the chair and prepared to intervene to prevent the collision, but there was no need. Jasper pinned Mulder with a glare and the dog stumbled over his own feet, as if sensing some invisible force field emanating from the cat. It was nothing more than the usual sheer arrogance the feline species all seemed to possess. Despite Mulder being the alpha of our home for his entire life, he appeared to be questioning where he sat in that hierarchy as he came to a stop about six inches from Jasper.

I let out a breath of relief while they faced off. Even though Mulder was bigger and had seniority, he was unwilling to take on the newcomer.

Gran finally spoke. "Well, who is this little fella?"

I cringed when she used the sing-song baby talk Jasper had informed me he wouldn't tolerate.

"I'm sorry." My comment was meant to temper Jasper. I feared he'd retaliate by jamming a claw into her ankle or through her thin linen pants. Instead, he jumped on her lap.

"For what?" she asked. "I think you owe Mulder the apology. You didn't tell him he was getting a sibling."

Jasper bumped his head against Gran's chin. "The grandmother may call me whatever she wants."

She didn't react to show she understood Jasper's words like I did. To her, he must've only meowed.

"I was apologizing because I should've asked you if the condo allowed cats." I threw out the excuse.

"Seriously? We're witches," Gran said. "Do you know how many cats are around here?"

"No." That made sense, but I hadn't noticed many other cats. Although, if they were smart, they wouldn't be outside when it was a bazillion degrees while the condos were comfortably air-conditioned.

Gran shrugged and continued to stroke Jasper's fur. He arched his back to press against her hand. "Me neither. I gave up keeping track of the cats a while ago. Where did you get him?"

Did I tell her the truth? She'd figure it out, eventually. I couldn't keep a secret from Gran. It was best to get it all out in a rush. "I found him outside the club when I took out a cocktail spell that went wrong and blew up. When I woke up, I discovered Jasper next to me and quickly realized we could understand each other."

I cringed, waiting for her to laugh, or declare I'd lost my mind, or make some—any—comment about my storytelling. Instead, she said, "So you found him by the dumpster? Poor little guy. He must be hungry."

Jasper turned to me and purred. "I knew I liked this witch."

"Gran. Did you hear me say I could talk to him? A cat?"

"For the last time, I don't need a hearing aid. I heard you the first time. Why would I think you being able to talk to a cat was any more unusual than James looking like he's already passed to the other side? Besides, I told you those charmed cocktails were nothing to mess with."

8

So far, I stunk as a sleuth. I hesitated to consider Burton as a suspect, and was slightly afraid to confront Gloria, so I questioned Samantha.

"I already established my alibi." She smiled smugly and tilted her head. "I was with Louis."

Another one of the married customers. Her story gave her an excuse to keep it a secret and also made it difficult to confirm.

"If you tell Vlad, I'll lose my job, witch," the vamp said. "You'd like that, wouldn't you?"

"No. I'd like to find Henry's killer, that's all." Unfortunately, I believed her. If she was going to lie, why would she use something she knew she'd get in trouble for when she could've made up any other excuse? Believe me, she had a lot of them.

I pulled out my little tablet from my apron and held my pencil by Samantha's name, unsure if I should eliminate her as a suspect. A gust of air confirmed the suspect in question had moved and was now peering over my shoulder.

"Go ahead. Cross off my name. Why would I stick him in the freezer?" She raised a perfectly plucked brow. "It would be a waste of a good meal. Even if old warlock blood is bitter."

I'd assumed the direct approach would work with her, since she often spoke before she thought, but I'd already had my doubts about her guilt. She was shady, and her vamp strength would enable her to lift a body into the freezer, but like she said, there wasn't an obvious motive.

Henry might have the ladies lining up at the retirement home, but he wasn't the type of guy Samantha would be interested in. He was unmarried, old, living on a fixed income, and had a style stuck in the 1970s.

Samantha huffed in impatience as I took longer to cross her name from my suspect list, merely to annoy her. Since I had no proper authority, her intense desire to be removed as a suspect was suspicious. I was only trying to do right by Henry and clear my name.

The vamp tapped my tablet to get my attention,

as if I wasn't already acutely aware of her hovering presence. "Didn't you see that bruise on Henry's head? Who could hit someone that hard?" She inclined her head toward the bar.

I thought perhaps a vampire could, but I didn't say as much because I knew what she was implying. "I don't think it was Burton," I said.

She put her hands on her narrow hips. "Oh, of course you don't. Because you're all buddy-buddy with him. Aren't you like his little protégé?"

"No, he's just my friend."

"And I'm not, or else you wouldn't have turned me in to Vlad." She pushed out her lip in a pout. "Do you plan to run to him now to tell him what I told you about Louis?"

I rolled my eyes as I wondered, once again, if maturity slowed for vampires because of their immortality. "No. For the last time, I didn't mean to turn you in. I didn't even know the guy was married."

Her smile was slow and predatory. "Aren't they always?" And with that, she turned to walk away.

"Wait, Samantha." Perhaps her nosiness could be helpful to me. "What about Gloria? Was she here that night?"

She shrugged and resumed walking; clearly, she'd lost interest. "Nope. I don't remember seeing her. Why don't you ask her for her alibi? Guess you wouldn't since she's a witch. I'm sure you all stick together. It's just the vamps you have it out for."

"It wasn't her." Burton said each word slowly, with emphasis.

I squeaked. "Gosh, Burton, do you have to sneak up on me like that?" Apparently, everyone else felt like they were doing a better job at sleuthing than me. "How do you know it wasn't Gloria?"

"I just do," he said.

I narrowed my gaze at him. Why would he stick up for Gloria? He wouldn't give up any details if she was one of his clients for who-knows-what dirty deeds. "Then who killed Henry?"

"I don't know. There are customers waiting." He returned to the bar.

He and Samantha had squashed my brief investigation just like that. Maybe they were trying to lead me to another path to protect themselves or someone else. Maybe they just didn't care for witches or Henry. But I did.

My investigation needed to expand outside of the club. I wasn't sure where to start, but perhaps Gran, or someone else at the retirement condominiums, could tell me more about Henry's usual routine. Fran probably had it documented somewhere. Guess there were benefits to living with so many busy bodies.

Luckily for me—or not—I'd get to see most of

the local witches together at Henry's wake. They were holding the event here at Night Moves, which would speed up my interviewing process.

All the television murder shows Gran watched claimed the killer often liked to return to the scene of the crime, or the funeral. The wake would be the perfect place to try out my confession cocktail. I hadn't made it since I was a teenager trying to get Ava to admit the truth about the dent in mom and dad's car. Even then, I couldn't get my sister to drink it—she never trusted my charms—but it turned out her best friend, Grace, had been the one to blame. To this day, I wasn't sure if the charm had worked, or if Grace had just fessed up. She was like Ava, with her sense of propriety.

AFTER MENTIONING MY DILEMMA, JASPER INSISTED he could be helpful with the case. Since I was coming up empty so far, and it appeared as if James had ghosted the investigation or perhaps forgotten he'd offered to do it, I gave in. Our new partnership risked irritating Mulder. The two of them vied for attention like children and made it abundantly clear I was going to need to develop a lot more patience.

I worried Jasper might get stepped on at the club

with the liquor flowing and a plethora of oldsters without stellar vision, so I insisted he stay in my tote bag.

The cantankerous feline only agreed to the ride in the bag looped over my arm because he was more concerned about being fussed over. He might tolerate Gran, but she seemed to be an exception, and the only one he permitted fawning over him with baby talk. There was nothing like a black cat to get all the witches fussing.

The room Night Moves set up for the wake had people packed shoulder to shoulder. They either loved Henry, or Vlad's promise of free food and drinks. It was the least he could do to maintain his loyal customer base, since they had found the warlock dead on the premises.

I weaved my way through the witches and warlocks, accidentally bumping my bag into people and furniture until Jasper's complaints gained my attention. "Could you watch where you're going?"

"Oh, I'm sorry. I wasn't paying attention," I said, hoping no one noticed me talking to my tote bag.

"Obviously." He popped his silky black head from the bag to swat at my arm.

"Oh, who do we have here?" Charlotte descended upon my tote while Jasper attempted to sink back into its depths. Too late.

Like a fussing free-for-all, she shoved her hand into the bag, heedless of whether she might gain a scratch, to scoop Jasper up under his front legs.

"I wouldn't do that if I were you. He might bite." My words fell upon deaf ears. Literally. Charlotte wasn't wearing her hearing aids. Although, if the enamored look on her face was any sign, I don't think my warning would've done any good. Jasper's eyes narrowed to slits, and he flattened his ears as she planted kiss after kiss on top of his head.

Several other witches noticed Jasper and created a small circle around us. They all clamored closer to see him and shoved me out of the way until it left me standing on the outside of the huddle holding my empty bag. As I looked around the room, I realized it wasn't just the cat that was out of the bag.

My confession cocktails were a tremendous hit, especially since I said it was a drink in Henry's honor and neglected to mention the nature of the charm. My truth, along with all the other truths that were pouring out from loose lips like water from a faucet, would come out later. Most of the conversation was about things no one ever wanted to hear. Learning who waxed what, who slept with who, which witch had plastic surgery on what, was unpleasant. Even more unpleasant was that no one was talking about Henry's murder. Fran was writing furiously in her little tablet, bound to have enough material for the rest of the year.

Gran came to stand beside me and pulled a flask out of her pocket. She knew me way too well, and despite what she said, she didn't trust my cocktails all that much either. "I see you dug out that old charmed confession cocktail again," she said. "You remember it didn't work the first time with Ava?"

I shrugged. "I thought it couldn't hurt." Well, I hoped it wouldn't hurt anything or anyone. After all, it had been awhile since I'd stirred up this brew.

She tucked the flask away who knows where in her skin tight outfit and tugged at my arm. "Come on. Now's our chance to go over to the table with the display of Henry's memorabilia and photos. We might learn something there."

I pointed to the crowd of witches. "But they have Jasper. It's like they've never seen a cat before."

She waved me off. "He'll be fine. He might act like he hates it, but I'm guessing he loves the attention. Let's go check out Henry's stuff while everyone's distracted."

After several quick steps, we stood beside the table featuring photos of Henry. Gran took my hand and squeezed it. Despite her nonchalant attitude, I think she needed this time to say goodbye. The photos confirmed the warlock had maintained his seventies-style mustache for some time. The clothing styles and hairstyles might have changed over time in the photos, but the mustache remained evergreen.

By the time I pushed my way back through the witches and reclaimed Jasper, he looked desperate. "It's about time you rescued me."

He played up his outrage, but I could tell it hadn't been all terrible. He'd barely stopped purring before I snagged him. Gran was right; he enjoyed the attention. His irritability was an act. Deep down, he was a softie.

The liquor was kicking in with the remaining crowd, so the volume was increasing. By now, I'd had about enough of the wake, but to pacify Jasper and allow him to think he was doing his part, I agreed to do one quick spin around the room before we left. A nice hot shower followed by a cup of tea was calling me, and I had to work the early shift tomorrow.

Jasper scanned the room as I walked. He dipped down into the bag anytime he felt as if someone was giving him more than a courtesy glance to avoid another fuss fest. "Wait," he hissed.

I was just circling past the table of photos and memorabilia when I heard his muffled request. This area of the room was opening up more, since people were trickling out into the primary area of the club to the dance floor.

I sighed as exhaustion weighed on me. "What? We're almost done."

"No. Stop right here." Jasper had his paws on the edge of the bag and was staring at the photos. "Who is that in the picture?"

"What picture? There's an entire table of them." I spread my arms to illustrate the volume of items on the table.

"The guy with the mustache. The one who's in most of the photos." He swatted my arm.

I rolled my eyes. "Funny. That's Henry."

Jasper's gaze shot to me. "The murdered guy?"

"Of course. Why do you think we're here?" I sighed in exasperation. "Are we done now? My feet are killing me and I still have to walk home."

"How was I supposed to know what he looked like? You never showed me a picture. I see lots of humans. Most of them look the same. But that's him. That's both of them." Jasper's voice rose with excitement and he bounced in the bag.

I frowned. "What are you talking about? That's who?"

"The guy with the mustache, Henry, and that other guy with him in most of the pictures," he said as his voice rose.

I scanned the photos. The person accompanying Henry most frequently was Fred. I picked up a framed photo of Henry and Fred with their hands clasped, raising a paper bingo card in victory. "Who? This guy? Fred?" I tapped his image on the frame. "What about him?"

"He's the other human that was with Henry that morning," Jasper said with a nod. "He's always with him in the morning at the club."

"So? They always hung out together," I said.

Jasper sighed as if he were explaining to a simpleton. "Those two humans, the ones you call Henry and Fred."

I nodded.

"Every morning they'd go into the club before it opened. I'd wait outside," he said. "After they met me, and realized how absolutely adorable I was, of course, they'd bring me food when they left. The day I met you when you collapsed from the utter joy of discovering me, only one guy left the club, and he left in a hurry. So quick that he didn't stop to give me anything to eat. That's why I was out there when you came. I was still waiting for something to eat."

I gasped. "Are you certain you saw them both go to the club that morning?"

Jasper frowned. His whiskers twitched as he concentrated. "Yes."

"Could they understand you, like I can?"

"No. What does that have to do with anything?" He rolled his eyes.

"You're right." Part of me felt relief because I didn't want someone else to understand Jasper like I could. The idea made me feel like our relationship wouldn't be as special.

But I needed to focus. What mattered now was that it placed Fred at the scene of the crime. Both men went into the club with Henry still alive, but Fred was the only one that left.

9

"I'm so sorry for your loss, Fred," I said.

The aging warlock stood in the doorway of his condominium, looking more unkempt than I'd ever seen him. I would've guessed he'd overdid it at the wake, but I'd seen him leave early. Jasper and I had stopped by his condo last night after we left, but no one answered. Since it was later in the evening, and most, if not all, of the residents of the condominiums who were home were asleep, it didn't surprise me.

I couldn't divulge my suspicions that Fred murdered Henry to anyone yet. At least not until I'd investigated it myself. How was I to accuse him of murdering his best friend? To say I knew he was guilty because my talking cat saw the two men at the club that morning? No one would believe me, especially because I was a much more likely suspect. Plus, there might be a logical explanation.

Fred continued to stand silently in the doorway, squinting at me as if he wasn't sure what to do next.

"Do you mind if I come in?" I smiled and hoped this wasn't a bad idea. I hadn't even had time to talk to Gran about how Jasper had placed him at the scene of the crime. She was sleeping when I came home last night and still this morning. I knew her exhaustion would be more likely a result of the dancing rather than drinking. The old witch could really shake her booty.

Fred frowned, but didn't seem to think of a reason to refuse me. "I suppose." He ran a hand over his head and glanced over his shoulder. "I haven't cleaned up."

"That's okay. I just want to chat with you for a minute," I said. Fred saying he hadn't cleaned up was an understatement. Both he and his place were a wreck. I wrinkled my nose at the odor and located the overflowing trash can as the source. That, or something crusted over on the dishes piled in the sink, or the ones on the counter.

Fred stared at me. Gone was the gregarious socialite. Perhaps he wasn't whole without his sidekick. I felt bad having to question him, but we should leave no stone unturned. Since James Stone hadn't looked under any stones, and evidence was piling up, that left me.

The jab from Jasper shoving his claw through the bag to my leg reminded me of the purpose of my visit. "There's someone I'd like you to meet," I said and set my bag down. I assumed it would be hard to make a regal exit out of an old tote bag, but Jasper did his best and strutted out with his tail held high.

"Oh." A slight smile tugged at the corner of Fred's lip. "That looks like a friendly cat."

Jasper scowled when Fred didn't recognize him. The cat's sleek, black coat and piercing golden eyes contributed to his handsome appearance, but the unique thing about him was his personality. Except from what I could tell, I was the only one who received the full benefit—and punishment—of all of that.

"This is Jasper. I thought you might've seen him before at Night Moves." I studied Fred for a reaction.

He cocked his head and looked at Jasper. Recognition dawned on Fred's face. "You know what? I think I have. He hangs out behind the club. Did you find him there? Henry or I often brought him a treat or other leftovers." Fred returned his attention to me with more wariness in his expression.

Of course, he wouldn't consider that Jasper

might've seen something that morning, or that the cat would've told me anything to implicate him in Henry's murder. I'd have to do a little more covert convincing to get him talking.

"I often work the early shift." I knelt to stroke Jasper, then raised my gaze to meet Fred's. "You were there that morning." This wasn't a lie. I didn't have to say I knew this because Jasper told me. I was usually the first one in the club each morning, so it made perfect sense I might've seen him leaving and he didn't see me.

"You saw me," he said. His face paled, and he sunk into the couch. The newspapers and discarded food wrappers littering the cushions crunched when he sat upon them. I was happy he'd lowered himself closer to my level. It was only after I'd knelt that I realized it put me at a distinct disadvantage if Fred was dangerous or retaliated to keep me quiet.

I paused, weighing my next words. Catching him off guard had given me the advantage in the conversation so far. I hadn't actually said I saw him that morning, or that I knew anything he might've done, but I nodded to keep him talking. And talk he did.

His face crumbled like the wrappers surrounding him, and he dropped his head into his hands. "It was an accident. I should've said something then, but after I tried to help. Well, it made it worse. Then more time went by, and it made me look guiltier. I'm a terrible friend."

I scooped up Jasper and stood to loom over Fred. "You killed Henry. I think that makes you much crueler than a terrible friend," I said. "A poor friend might forget a birthday, or say something inappropriate, but not kill someone."

He straightened, and his eyes grew wide. "For goddess' sake, no. I didn't kill Henry! He was my best friend."

"Then how come he was dead when you left?" I was pushing my luck with this question, and I never had much luck to start with. Who knew what Fred was capable of, and here I was provoking him. Jasper might have the customary nine lives, but I didn't think I did. Still, I had to know if Fred was responsible.

Fred sighed and reached down to the corner of the cushion. I tensed, but he only retrieved a rumpled picture of Henry and himself. He smoothed the worn photo out with his thumb. "I miss him," he said and wiped the corner of his eye. "We've been friends for the last thirty years. I never thought he'd be the first to go. Guess I didn't want to consider it."

He met my gaze. "It started with a stupid argument." He grimaced. "Well, argument is a strong word. It was more like a disagreement. We both were interested in Charlotte and were arguing over who would be the better man. That there was even an argument about this is ridiculous because it wouldn't be up to either of us. Charlotte was the only one who could decide that." He shrugged. "But, we were going back and forth about who she should choose."

Jasper opened his mouth, most likely to claim he was right, but I shushed him. It was hard enough for me to keep quiet this long, but if I could do it to keep Fred talking, Jasper could too.

Fred stared at the photo with a hint of a smile. "I knew he had me when he brought up his dancing skills. He could really cut a rug back in the day. So, when he said he'd be a better dancer and could whisk Charlotte off her feet, I claimed he no longer had it in him. He accepted the challenge. I reached over the counter to look for where to turn on the music. I knocked over some spelling ingredients while I was searching for the blasted button."

He took a deep breath before continuing. "When I finally got the music on, Henry jumped from the barstool, and headed for the dance floor." He hung his head. "His pants must've caught on the chair, or he lost his balance, because he stumbled and went down. Then he didn't get up. Who would've thunk it? Over a woman."

That couldn't be the entire story. "But there was magic residue on him," I pressed.

Fred shook his head. "I know. I thought maybe I could save him. It was just a fall. He hit his head hard. But surely that wouldn't be enough to kill a warlock? I had some old spelling materials in my jacket, but I worried they might've been no good, probably expired. So, I looked around for a first aid kit, but I found the spelling and charm stuff stashed behind the bar that I'd bumped when I turned on the music." He frowned. "What's that stuff doing there, anyway? I never even heard of a few of those potions."

I waved him off to avoid deterring the topic to me and my secret ingredients.

"But nothing worked. I was flustered and wasn't sure exactly what measurements I was using. In fact, some mixtures backfired. I don't know if I combined the wrong stuff, or it was because mine was old. I don't know and probably never will. But I couldn't help him." His face fell.

I hated to push him, but I needed the rest of the story. "Were you afraid you'd get in trouble for being there?"

He shook his head. "We'd been coming there

early for years. I'm sure Vlad suspected us, but we disturbed nothing and always left cash in the tip jar. Neither of us can stay up late anymore, and the noise in the club is too loud. We missed hanging out there. So we'd go to the club to have coffee and conversation."

Vlad allowing two old warlocks alone in the club was almost more of a surprise than Fred being responsible for Henry's death. Maybe I was judging too much on appearances. There was one last thing that still made little sense. "Why would you put him in the freezer?"

Once Fred started confessing, he couldn't stop. "Because I thought it would help preserve him until I figured out a spell to bring him back." Fred's pain-filled gaze met mine. "But I figured nothing out. Reviving after death, or reincarnation, has never happened, at least not in any spell book I could find. I didn't want him to come back as a zombie, if that's even possible. I asked around to see if we could bring him back as a vampire or a werewolf. You know, without explaining who I was asking for, or why. I even thought about asking that creepy bartender, but I couldn't get up the nerve to talk to him. But it didn't matter because everyone told me no. And I'm not so sure Henry would've been too happy if I could've done it, anyway. He loved being a warlock."

He dropped his head into his hands and sobbed big, loud, messy tears. I reached to pat his leg. "It's going to be okay."

It was the most comfort I could provide because I did not know what was in store for Fred.

❧ 10 ❧

My shift was winding down. It was early yet, so the club wasn't that busy. Gran swiveled on the bar stool and reached for the charmed bodacious bikini cocktail I'd made at her request. Since my previous attempt at something new exploded, and I could never forget what I'd heard from the confession cocktail, I'd been hesitant to create new drinks. That was exactly why she'd ordered one. She wasn't one to let me dwell on my insecurities. That, and she was always game to try any beverage that included a splash of an allure charm.

I hesitated before extending the frosted glass topped with a tiny umbrella. "Are you positive you want this? It's a new recipe."

Gran pulled the drink from my grasp, took a long swallow, and then smacked her lips in satisfaction.

"Why not? I like to live dangerously. Besides, we're celebrating. You solved your first case."

"I wouldn't say that." I shrugged, but ducked my head to hide my smile. Discovering the truth behind Henry's death secretly pleased me.

"Wouldn't say what?" She turned to the side, propped an elbow on the bar, and tossed one calf over her other knee so she could survey the men in the club. Her wedge sandal dangled from her toes as she bounced her leg.

"Either. That I solved it, or that it was my first case," I said.

"I have to agree with you there," Jasper grumbled from the cabinet under the bar. When Gran said she was coming for one last toast to Henry and to celebrate clearing my name, Jasper insisted he should come, too.

Gran tapped the bar. "Jasper agrees with me."

"He's not agreeing with you. If you could understand his meows, you'd realize that he thinks he deserves all the credit since he picked Fred out in the picture."

She lifted her glass. "Well, you two make an excellent team."

I ran a hand over my hair. Joe had tried and failed to cover up the streak I'd earned when I gained the ability to talk to Jasper. The hairdresser said he'd seen nothing like it and that it might be permanent. "I didn't really solve it since Fred confessed, and saying it's my first case means there's going to be more. Most likely, it's my last case unless you expect to find more dead bodies."

"It might surprise you, but there's always something going on around here," she said as her attention locked on a man at the other end of the bar.

"What's going to happen to Fred?" It had been a few days since the story broke, first in the Willow Words, then the town. I'd given Fran the scoop first to get her to agree not to share any more pictures or stories about me without my permission.

"It was an accident, but still, he panicked, hid the body, and used magic on Henry," Gran said. "The magic may have done more harm than good, but we'll never know. They kicked him out of the condominiums for his dishonesty. Maybe if he'd alerted someone sooner, they could have done something for Henry. We witches have to stick together." She shrugged. "What happens to Fred is in the hands of the police now. You did your job. As I said, you might have a new career as a private investigator."

"The only thing I'm good at is being a waitress—if that. I'm not so sure how I'd be as an investigator." Truth be told, I'd probably done a better job solving the case than I had with my charmed cocktails as of late. However, Gran looked like she was enjoying the new one I'd created, and it seemed to work. I'd caught a few men glancing in her direction.

"Stop being so modest. It doesn't suit you." Gran stood from the stool, taking her cocktail and leaving a wet ring on the bar. "Now, if you'll excuse me, I see a few warlocks who might want to buy a lady a drink." She winked before walking away with an extra sway to her hips. Her tight skirt clung to her butt enough to leave little to the imagination.

I shook my head and smiled. It was nice to be with Gran. She might exasperate me, but she was fun to be around and good for my self-confidence.

An investigator? Me? Right. Although, if I thought about it, I'd done more than James Stone in solving Henry's case. No one had seen the pale private eye since that day. He was deep undercover, or he forgot about agreeing to investigate Henry's death.

I leaned on the bar and looked at Burton. It relieved me that he had nothing to do with Henry's death. I never thought he did, but well, you never know what some people are capable of. With Burton, I hoped I'd never find out.

"I've had enough. I'm ready to go home," Jasper piped up from under the counter.

I bent, opened the cabinet door under the bar, and came face to whiskers with a cranky-looking kitty. I still didn't know what went wrong with that charmed cocktail that enabled me to understand him or if this was a permanent situation. "Be quiet. You know Vlad will toss you out if he discovers you in the club. I only have an hour left for my shift. Take a nap."

"Fine. It's insulting that you shoved me under the bar when I'm the genuine hero in this investigation." He hissed. "I'm not sure how much rest I'll get with the volume in this place."

I raised a brow. "It's better than hanging out by the dumpster, isn't it?"

He ignored me, walked in a circle, and curled up on my jacket. "Wake me when you're ready to go. Don't forget to get something special for my dinner. You never would've figured out what happened to Henry if it wasn't for me."

I smiled. "You're right, and so was Gran. We make a pretty wonderful team."

He cracked an almond-shaped eye, and I caught a hint of a smile. "If you say so."

I closed the cabinet and surveyed the rapidly filling club. If not for the cocktails, other people came here hoping to grace the same stage that launched a handful of singing sensations back in the day. I interrupted my mindless perusal of the crowd when I spotted a man hunched over in hushed conversation with Burton at the end of the bar. I frowned. Talent wasn't always necessary for a rise to fame or fortune. Some of them made a deal with the devil, or should I say, one of the devil's associates.

It was likely that they didn't always make the connection at first. At least, that's what I assumed. Over the last few days, I'd allowed my overactive imagination to fill in the blanks of the things I didn't know about Burton, which was a lot.

I sighed, thinking of Henry again. I hadn't known him for long, but he'd affected my perception of the world. Most people were all about today and not thinking about tomorrow. Paranormals lived a long time, but not forever. Some seemed to forget about their mortality.

Warm breath on my shoulder confirmed Burton had come up behind me. I'd gotten better at detecting him before he startled any more years from my life.

"Any potential tonight?" I slipped my tray from under the counter, wiped it with a cloth, and winked at him. Ever since I discovered he was a demon, I liked to play this game to see if the man of stone might crack one day. There had to be a sense of humor underneath that unyielding exterior.

Instead, he met me with his usual blank stare and didn't even raise a brow. I'd shared his secret life with my sister, Ava. Maybe she'd worry less about me directly and worry more about the company I kept instead. I hoped it read as, "See? I could be worse."

I scanned the bar. "How about that dude? He looks like he would enjoy an eternity festering in the heat of the underbelly."

Without thought, I continued, "How about Gloria over there?"

Oh no. I cringed, remembering that Gran had said Fred was no longer living at the condos, which meant there was an opening, two if you considered Henry's condo. I could only hope they wouldn't fill either of those with Gloria.

"She's been complaining up a storm tonight. Perhaps she's looking for a heated time out..." When I nodded toward Gloria, I might've actually detected something from Burton. Was that a response from the man of stone?

It looked like distaste and a little... could it be anger? Even though this was the first time I'd sparked his attention, I found this little acknowledgment of his disturbing. I had no desire to fan that fire and find out what he was made of. I needed to step away —time to do my rounds.

I slipped the tray under my arm and walked through the tables, stacking empty glasses as I passed them. I gathered drink orders for my return trip. Not for the first time, I wondered what prompted Vlad to think having a demon posted in the bar was a good idea. Or perhaps Burton came as a package deal since I'd heard, or maybe assumed, that the club was at the Underworld entrance. It's not like they could move the underbelly of eternal purgatory. Surely nothing else could happen since I was friends—or at least I thought I was—with a demon.

If I'm honest, in some ways, I was glad he was here. I hoped that besides escorting people in through the fiery gates; he was also keeping whoever was down there from getting out. We had enough riffraff without recycling more evil entities. Bad boys were never good at cleaning up after themselves and left a gigantic mess and a small tip. No, thank you.

For now, I was happy enough to be staying in Gran's condo with a talking cat and a too-furry-for-the-Florida-heat dog, a new hairdresser on speed dial, and one solved crime under my belt. Now that Henry's death was explained, I could enjoy the rest of my working vacation while things were quiet. Knowing me, things wouldn't be quiet for long.

Want to find out what happens next for Marissa?

A struggling witch. A cocktail of confusion. A rink full of officials carrying her friend away for her own mistake.

Hexes, Highballs & Hockey is the top-shelf second book in the Charmed Cocktail Cozy mystery series.

MARISSA HALE IS A WALKING MESS. TIRED OF BEING nothing more than a mediocre witch, the aspiring mixologist is desperate to shake up her image. But outing herself for illicit magic is a no-go, even if her simple stain-removing spell sends her friend away in chains.

Anxious to clear her pal's name without implicating herself, Marissa fears her double-duty misfire may have also skyrocketed a hockey player to instant fame. But as she and her chatty cat dig deeper, she's stunned to discover the superstar athlete is keeping a shocking celestial secret...

Will Marissa free the wrongfully accused and fess up before she's next in the penalty box?

Magic, Mimosas & Mistletoe is the high-spirited third book in the Charmed Cocktail Cozy mystery series.

She doesn't see dead people, but her dog does. Can the spirits help her solve the mystery and save Christmas?

MARISSA HALE IS EXCITED TO VISIT HER FRIEND Grace's new Inn. But the twinkly lights attached to the inheritance are frightful, and finding a dead body in the poinsettias resembling one of Santa's fabled elves is not delightful. The death of Grace's aunt was already suspicious, is someone trying to scare Grace into selling the Kringle Inn?

Grace's bloodline is the magic mainline for keeping the yuletide spirit alive, and losing the Inn could mean the end of Christmas. The clues to both deaths may reside with the spirits of the Inn, but Marissa's dog is the only one who can see them.

Does Marissa stand a ghost of a chance of solving this mystery to save Christmas?

WILL YOU HELP OTHER READERS FIND THIS BOOK?

Thank you for reading my story! I love sharing my characters and their fun adventures. I hope they bring you as much joy reading them as they give me writing them.

If you have enjoyed this story, it would be fantastic if you would leave a review.

Reviews are magical! They help my books get noticed and bring them to the attention of other readers who may enjoy them.

You can leave a review for Curses, Cats & Corpses right here.

Have a magical day!

Maureen

Half the time, we're writing the history of these Unknown paranormal species. That's what I do. I'm Violet. I don't have a reference book. I am the reference book.

The Enchantlings Series

This Urban Fantasy story features Hope, as she struggles to determine if her ability to infuse euphoria or despair with her touch makes her the devil's spawn or his exterminator.

Other Standalone Stories

Evil Speaks Softly

Fame came easily for Liv by following in the footsteps of the female writers in her family. The cycle repeated for decades...until Liv changed the story. Her villain doesn't like the revision—and he isn't a fictional character.

Till Death

To protect an innocent man, a dutiful wife challenges her vengeful husband...with disastrous results.

ABOUT THE AUTHOR

Just a small-town girl, M.L. Bonatch leads a double
life. She lives in a magical world, writing cozy paranormal mysteries and sweet, humorous paranormal
romance as M.L. Bonatch and urban fantasy as
Maureen Bonatch.

While she's not busy writing or doing nurse things,
she's a mom to her twin daughters, bicycling in the
beautiful woods of PA with her hubby, doing the
bidding of a feisty Shih Tzu, and dancing as much as
possible. She believes music can be paired with every
mood, laughter is contagious, and that caffeine and
wine are essential for survival.

Be the first to find out about book sales, new releases, and other fun stuff from her furry sidekick, Scruff, by signing up for her newsletter: https://www.maureenbonatch.com/free-book/

Find all Maureen's stories here: https://www.maureenbonatch.com/

Keep in touch with my magical world by following me everywhere.

a amazon.com/-/e/B0951C41XM

BB bookbub.com/authors/m-l-bonatch

f facebook.com/MLBonatch

twitter.com/mbonatch

instagram.com/mlbonatch.author

pinterest.com/maureenbonatch

GET YOUR FREE STORIES

Get several free short stories, including *Spells, Spirits & Stiffs*, when you sign up for my newsletter. It's free to sign up, and you can opt-out anytime. Copy and paste this link to get more magical stories: https://www.maureenbon atch.com/free-book/

SPELLS, SPIRITS & STIFFS, A CHARMED Cocktail Cozy Mystery

What's worse than a bunch of elderly witches in provocative Halloween costumes? One dead one.

HI, I'M MARISSA HALE. I SHOULD'VE KNOWN THAT mixing cocktails, costumes, and meddling would end with a corpse.

One of the best things about living at the Willow Hill retirement condos with Gran is that Halloween is a month-long celebration. One of the worst things is that the elderly witches gorge on more gossip than treats. These magic mavens love to get the scoop, as long as they aren't the headline.

When the informant for the condo newsletter ends up dead at the Halloween party, there are more suspects than skeletons in these closets. While I'm trying to figure out whodunit to the hostess most likely to be stabbed, the thirsty rambunctious residents raid my charmed cocktail station.

My furry sleuthing side-kicks and I might need a few tricks to ensure that things don't get even more deadly...

Join my exclusive group- Must Love Magic:
https://www.facebook.com/groups/630494098126926

SNEAK PEEK AT BOOK 2

Hexes, Highballs & Hockey
A Charmed Cocktail Cozy
Book 2

When my specialty drink was returned for the second time, it was time to intervene. The frilly cocktail waitress dress swayed with the swing of my hips.

"Is there something wrong with the drink?" I eyed the slender mortal man brave enough to approach gin-and-juice Gloria, Night Moves queen customer complainer and mega witch. The later club hours tended to deter mortals when the supernatural folk let their glamour fade. Mortals realized magic existed but were only willing to stray so far from their reality.

The man shook his head while leaning to see past

me. "I was hoping to talk to the bartender." He lifted his drink with a shaky hand, rattling the ice cubes.

I relaxed. It wasn't my drink. "Listen ..."

"Steve."

"Well, Steve, Burton's busy." Usually, as long as the mortals minded their own business, the paranormal minded theirs but throw in too much booze, and there were often poor decisions and a lot of cleaning up and explaining to do.

"You wouldn't understand. You're not a mortal." The man ran his gaze over my hair, settling on the black streak.

Mortals didn't have to worry about a misspell showing up as a black streak like witches did. I envied the uniform coloring of his perfect coif. My misguided spelling attempts had left my hair with a shameful streak and a lot of frizz to advertise my magical mistakes. "The drink was okay, then?"

"The best highball I ever had. If he won't come over, can I go talk to him?" He stood, swaying on his feet.

I braced a hand on his chest to steady him and pause his pursuit. "Only if you're going to ask him which tequila he recommends." I didn't want to scare this guy, but he needed to be scared. Burton was my friend in a warped kind of way, but he was also a demon.

The guy's eyes widened, and a twinge of sobriety must've made him pause. "Will he send me to hell?"

"Sugar, look around. You're already there." I held out my arms to encompass the club. "Do you see anything else here besides monsters?" With a flick of my finger, I let the glamour fall away. It was easy to accept that weres, vamps, witches, and about every other creature under the sun were mixed in among the mortals when they looked almost like everyone else. It wasn't easy when you got a glimpse of their true nature.

I dropped my arms and let the curtain of glamour return to cloak the club. The dude's face paled, and my quick reflexes caught his glass before it hit the floor. A few ice cubes toppled over the side.

Grace came to stand beside me as we watched him stumble toward the door. "Marissa Hale, did you scare another customer away?"

I'd done it before when a patron got too drunk or annoying. Grace just didn't know this one was being too stupid. "At least he had already paid his tab before leaving."

Grace folded her arms over the tray she clutched against her chest. "Burton's not going to be happy."

I shrugged. "It's not like you can tell. Burton doesn't seem to have any emotions." I picked the cash off the table and counted it. "Besides, this guy left a hefty tip." I handed her half.

"See, and people say you have no real heart." Grace draped her arm around my waist. Her height prevented her from reaching my shoulders.

"They don't give me enough credit. Make sure you put in a good word with my sister. Ava never believes that I have the best intentions." My twin sister, Ava, was the better person out of the two of us and was temporarily here in Florida for work.

Grace looked at me. "Do you have plans for your day off tomorrow?"

I scoured my brain. There had to be something better to say than a big fat nothing after my hair appointment with Joe other than returning to the Willow Hill witch and warlock retirement condominium where I lived with Gran.

But with Gran off on a cruise, those retired busybodies were far too interested in the shenanigans that seemed to follow me. Especially since one of the first things I did after starting this job was find a dead body. Then a charmed cocktail gone rogue somehow gave me the ability to talk to Jasper, the stray cat I was forced to adopt. I had to. He wouldn't shut up until I did. Plus, he was kind of cute, although Mulder, my Shih Tzu, wasn't keen on the addition. "Umm, not yet."

"Great! Brian came down with something, so you can go to the hockey game with me."

Grace hurried away because she knew I would refuse. Not only because I preferred talking to animals or oldsters over anyone else, but also because I had no interest in hockey. But I didn't want to let her down, either. "Sure. Why not."

PICK UP YOUR COPY TODAY TO KEEP READING *Hexes, Highballs & Hockey. The top-shelf second book in the Charmed Cocktail Cozy mystery series.*